leapfrog Fairy Tales

Chicken Licken

retold by Elizabeth Rogers

Illustrated by Andy Rowland

W
FRANKLIN WATTS
LONDON·SYDNEY

First published in 2009 by
Franklin Watts
338 Euston Road
London
NW1 3BH

Franklin Watts Australia
Level 17/207 Kent Street
Sydney
NSW 2000

Text © Franklin Watts 2009
Illustration © Andy Rowland 2009

A CIP catalogue record for this book is available
from the British Library.

ISBN 978 0 7496 8607 9 (hbk)
ISBN 978 0 7496 8613 0 (pbk)

Series Editor: Jackie Hamley
Series Advisor: Dr Barrie Wade
Series Designer: Peter Scoulding

Printed in China

Franklin Watts is a division of
Hachette Children's Books,
an Hachette UK company.
www.hachette.co.uk

One day, an acorn fell on the head of a silly chick called Chicken Licken.

"Oh no!" she yelped. "The sky is falling in! I must tell the king!"

Off she scurried, and soon she met Henny Penny.

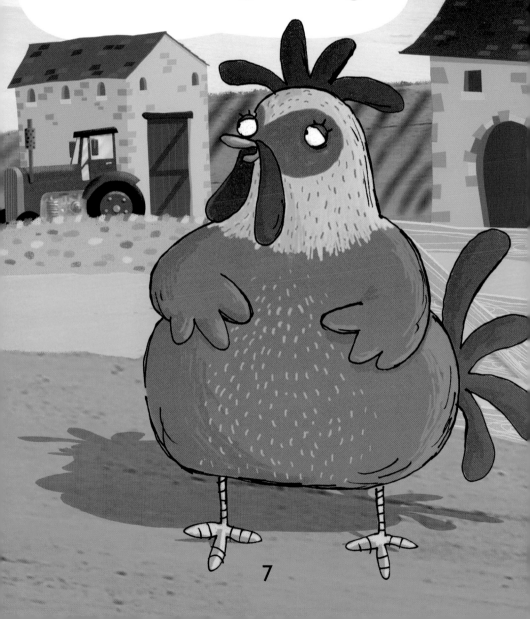

"Where are you going?" asked Henny Penny.

7

"The sky is falling in!" cried Chicken Licken. "Some of it fell on my head! I'm going to tell the king."

9

"I will come, too," clucked Henny Penny.

11

They soon met Ducky Lucky.

"The sky is falling in!"
cried Henny Penny.
"We're going to tell
the king."

"I will come, too,"
quacked Ducky Lucky.

16

Down the lane, they met Goosey Loosey.

"Where are you three going?" asked Goosey Loosey.

19

"The sky is falling in!"
cried Ducky Lucky. "We're
going to tell the king."

"I will come, too,"
honked Goosey Loosey.

By the hedge, they met
Foxy Loxy.

"Where are you four delicious birds going?" asked Foxy Loxy.

"The sky is falling in!"
cried Chicken Licken.
"We're off to tell the king!"

"Do you know the way?"
asked the cunning old fox.
"No!" said the four
silly birds.

"Let me show you,"
smiled Foxy Loxy,
licking his lips.

Foxy Loxy led the four birds to his den in the hedge. And the king never did hear about the sky falling in.

29

Puzzle 1

Put these pictures in the correct order.
Now tell the story in your own words.
What different endings can you think of?

Puzzle 2

calm   clever

foolish

sly   generous

cunning

wise   careful

silly

Choose the correct adjectives for each character. Which adjectives are incorrect? Turn over to find the answers.

Answers

Puzzle 1

The correct order is: 1d, 2e, 3a, 4c, 5f, 6b

Puzzle 2

Chicken Licken: the correct adjective is foolish

The incorrect adjectives are calm, clever

Foxy Loxy: the correct adjectives are cunning, sly

The incorrect adjective is generous

Ducky Lucky: the correct adjective is silly

The incorrect adjectives are careful, wise

Look out for Leapfrog fairy tales: